About the Author

Ethan Daniel James is the creator and host of the highly popular YouTube channel THE HONEST CARPENTER. A lifelong carpenter and tradesman, he now spends much of his time writing and teaching people how to work with their hands. He lives in Greensboro, North Carolina.

Visit the author at:
www.edanieljames.com
www.youtube.com/c/thehonestcarpenter

DUNgeoNWorLd

#1: One Hot Spark
#2: The Big Whiff
#3: Bang the War Drum
#4: The Royal Mess
#5: The Ghoul Ranch

DUNGEON WORLD

5

E. DANIEL JAMES

THE GHOUL RANCH

This is a work of fiction. Names, characters, places, and incidents either are the product of the author's imagination or are use fictitiously. Any resemblance to actual persons, living or dead, events, or locales is entirely coincidental.

Copyright © 2022 by E. Daniel James

All rights reserved. No part of this book may be reproduced or used in any manner without written permission of the copyright owner except for the use of quotations in a book review.

First paperback edition 2022
Book Illustrations by Michelle Nobles
ISBN 978-1-957349-08-4 (paperback)
ISBN 978-1-957349-09-1 (ebook)
Honest Carpenter Publishing
Visit the author online!
www.edanieljames.com

THE **GHOUL** RANCH

E. Daniel James
Illustrated by Michelle Nobles

1. Desperado

FRESH AIR.

Wide-open spaces.

That's what I crave!

Then again, you would too if you were buried under five hundred pounds of horse poop in the back of a dung cart!

"Thoracks, can I please get out now?" I shouted for the hundredth time.

The blue ogre in the front of the cart stopped whistling.

"Ehh...not yet. Still might be too dangerous out here."

"That's what you said three hours ago!"

"Just trying to play it safe, Spark."

I lay there in the poopy reek, breathing through my shirt. My head was swimming from dung fumes. My hip and back ached from the wooden cart bouncing over rocky ground. My skin itched and crawled.

I had never been this low before.

And that's saying something!

I mean, I had seen some rough times since I'd first shown up in Dungeonworld. I had slept on cold floors, worked crummy jobs, eaten stuff that would make a billy goat puke. But this... this was a different kettle of beans. Not only was I buried under a mountain of horse dung...

I was also an *outlaw*.

A renegade.
A desperado on the run!
And all because I'd told the Queen to lighten up a bit.

Looking back, I was sort of amazed I had ever wound up in the Queen's Palace to begin with. I mean, I'm just a *brunt*—a human servant in Dungeonworld. The scum at the bottom of the bucket.

See, ogres and goblins and trolls run this weird underground kingdom. But they need someone else to do all the dirty work. So, they snatch unsuspecting kids like me from the human world, bring us down here, and make us do the nasty jobs.

In my brief time in Dungeonworld, I had already worked as a blacksmith, toiled away in the sewer, and even served in the Army. But my best gig had come when the Queen herself had asked me to be her Jester.

I was born for that job!

I'm funny, charming, and I've got style

by the mile.

I spent all my time at the Palace pulling pranks, eating fancy food, and lying around on big, fluffy pillows. It was great!

All I had to do was keep the Queen laughing and keep my big mouth shut. But, as usual, that second part had proven difficult for me...

When the Queen asked me to sentence a bunch of innocent ghouls and goblins to punishment, I politely told her to get lost. Old Spark wasn't the guy for the job. (That's what they call me down here, by the way—*Spark*.)

Turns out the Queen doesn't like being told *No*.

The Ghoul Ranch

Go figure!

Things got pretty hairy for a moment there. The Queen handed me over to her Tormentor, a nut job named The Royal Pain. I thought I was mincemeat! But Thoracks pulled off a daring last-second rescue and got me out of the Palace in one piece.

At the time, I was counting my lucky stars.

But now, after hours of being buried in horse poop, jolting down every rocky road in Dungeonworld, I was at the end of my rope!

Something had to change...

~~~

I sucked my last lungful of stinky air.

"Thoracks, I can't take it anymore!" I shouted. "I'm coming out."

"Wouldn't do that if I were you," Thoracks replied. "It's pretty dangerous out here. You'll most likely be captured on the spot."

"I don't care!" I said. "I'd rather die in fresh air than live in poop!"

I furiously began digging my way out.

I felt like a tulip pushing its way up through wet, clammy soil. I scooped and scraped armloads of dung away. I kicked my legs and feet through brown mush. Little by little, I fought my way to the surface.

My head broke free!

I drew the longest, most refreshing breath of air I've ever tasted. It felt like I had just dug my way up from the grave! I pulled my arms out, wiped the gunk off my face, and looked around.

That was when I realized that Thoracks had been lying to me for the last fifty miles or more...

We were in the middle of what looked like a dark, quiet desert. Wispy bushes swished around us in the breeze. Dirt and rocks stretched for miles. A few tiny bats swooped lazily through the nighttime air.

That was it...

Not a soul in sight.

"We're in the middle of nowhere," I said.

Thoracks was chewing a long piece of straw.

"That's correct," he replied.

I surveyed the quiet landscape once more.
"And there's nobody out here," I added.
He spat the straw out into the dirt.
"Also correct."
I looked down at the festering dung cart I was in. I looked out at the miles and miles of wide-open dungeon that stretched out around us. Slowly, I began putting the pieces together in my head.
"You mean...you kept me down there in

poop for nothing?"

Thoracks shrugged.

"What can I say? I was enjoying the peace and quiet."

My head started to steam like a kettle.

Normally, if some other person had done this to me, I would have walloped them on the spot. No questions asked! But when the person in question is a four-hundred-pound ogre with bulging muscles and huge horns, you've got to think twice.

I decided just to let this one pass. It was actually pretty easy to do because I suddenly had so many questions flying through my head. The first one blurted right out of my mouth.

"Where are we?"

Thoracks waved a blue paw through the air.

"This, my boy, is the Great Dungeonworld Prairie!"

2. Firebugs

"**D**UNGEONWORLD HAS A prairie?!"

"Of course it does!" Thoracks said. "Dungeonworld's got everything the human world does. Maybe more, I reckon! Didn't I tell you that Dungeonworld was endless?"

"Yeah, but...I didn't think you were serious."

"Take a look around," Thoracks said. "This serious enough for you?"

I gazed out at the desolate landscape.

I could hardly believe what I was seeing!

Ever since I'd shown up in Dungeonworld weeks ago, I'd been surrounded by rocks and greasy monsters. I was always squeezing through narrow gates, running across bridges, and climbing winding staircases. The place felt like a cave with furniture.

But this...was the great wide open!

Cactus plants and prairie grasses sprawled out over rolling hills. Sharp mesas and plateaus stood out on the horizon. A gentle, slightly smoky breeze wafted over everything.

"What do you think?" Thoracks asked.

I struggled to find the words.

"It's actually kind of...beautiful."

"Darn tootin' it is!"

I was even more amazed when I looked up.

I couldn't see anything!

In Dungeonworld, there is always a stone ceiling or roof above you. If you jump too high, you'll probably bump your head on something. That's just part of living deep down underground.

But out here on the prairie, I couldn't see a single thing above us.

"Is there even a roof over this place?" I asked.

"Ahh, I reckon it's up there somewhere," Thoracks said. "Higher than you or I could ever go. Only the firebugs can fly that high. In fact, I reckon they're just now coming out...you see 'em?"

Even as I watched, the dark night began to sparkle. I had to rub my eyes! Hundreds of points of light began to blaze overhead. Thousands of them. They looked like...*stars*.

"Those are *firebugs?*" I asked

"Yep. Huge whompers too. Bigger than this cart! They hover around up there during the evenings. You'll see 'em moving about every now and then."

"Wow!"

I watched the distant firebugs drift lazily across the velvety dark above us. Eventually, my eyes drifted back down to the horizon. I peered out through the eerie glow that always hung about Dungeonworld, day and night.

"Where are we going?" I asked.

"A little place I know out on the prairie," Thoracks said. "A big ranch with lots of land. Old pal of my runs the place. I worked out there a few seasons when I was a lad."

This wasn't the first time Thoracks had talked about his old jobs. He'd been a soldier in the Dungeonworld Army once and even a guard in the Queen's Palace. But I was surprised to hear he'd worked on a ranch as well.

"You've worked all over the place, huh?" I asked.

"What can I say?" Thoracks replied. "I'm an ogre of parts."

I nodded wisely.

Thoracks had been the person responsible for finding me a job since I'd arrived in Dungeonworld. At first, I'd thought he was just a big bully. And don't get me wrong, he could still be a blue butthead at times!

But I was beginning to realize there was more to him than I thought.

I was *also* curious about this ranch.

"What do they do out here on the prairie?" I asked.

"Oh, all sorts of things," Thoracks said. "Train horses. Mend fences. Hunt flesh-eating birds. At this time of year, though, I reckon they'll be rounding up the winged boar."

"The *winged boar*," I said. "What's that?"

"What's it sound like? A pig with wings."

My head whipped around.

"So, pigs really *can* fly?!"

"In Dungeonworld, they can."

He gave the reins a pop and said "Yaaah." The sleepy mule plowed ahead in the traces. The clopping of its hooves made a hypnotic rhythm.

I watched tumbleweeds skitter by.

I listened to animals hooting in the dark.

It was sort of peaceful out here on the prairie. I'd spent so long getting chased from one place to the next in Dungeonworld, I'd forgotten what it was like to relax. This was a nice change of pace.

Eventually, I started to feel pretty sleepy. I leaned back on the cart bench and let my eyelids shut. My chin drooped to my chest. My mind drifted out over the dusty trail…

I woke up later with a snort and a jerk.

"Whozza, whuzza?"

The cart had come to a stop. Thoracks was nudging me.

"Wake up," he said. "We're here."

I sat up and rubbed the crust out of my eyes.

I looked around drowsily.

All I could see from the cart was more dust, darkness, and hills. My neck hurt from where I had slept on it wrong. I rubbed it, grimacing painfully.

"Where's *here?*" I said. "I don't see anything."

Thoracks yanked me upright in my seat.

"Down there, you dunce!"

He pointed directly over the mule's ears.

I squinted and peered down the long hill ahead of us.

Way, way out in the distance I saw torches flickering on the prairie. Ramshackle buildings and fences stretching out through the dark. I thought I could hear the sound of strange animals braying.

"Place seems sort of creepy," I said.

"It is," Thoracks replied.

He gripped the reins and started driving us forward again.

"Perk up and look spry, would you?" he

barked. "They can't stand a lazy sack of bones around here. And watch what you say too! They don't take kindly to a discouraging word."

"I'll do my best," I told him.

We went rolling down the hill.

Down to my new home on the range…

3. The Ghoul Ranch

UP AHEAD, THE road passed beneath a big, wooden arch. The arch was decorated with huge cow skulls, jangling bones, and rattlesnake skins.

A raw-headed vulture was biting its feathers on a nearby fence post. When it saw us, it let out a pterodactyl shriek.

Skrraawww!

It flapped its big wings and vanished into the night.

My teeth chattered a little.

"Who decorated this place?" I asked. "The grim reaper?"

"*Quiet*," Thoracks muttered.

He popped the reins and clucked his tongue. The mule lumbered forward. We rolled beneath the arch into a big dusty yard.

We passed a baggy scarecrow with hay coming out of its eyes and mouth. A rickety wooden windmill clacked and squeaked overhead. Watering troughs lay scattered here and there like coffins.

A tumbledown stone farmhouse with torches smoldering in brackets on the walls stood at the center of the yard. At first, I thought the place was abandoned. But then I saw something sitting in the shadows on the porch...

It looked like a *skeleton!*

I thought an old rancher had died and dried up right there on the porch. But, to my amazement, the skeleton coughed! A cloud of dust spewed from its mouth. It leaned forward, and I realized that the skeleton was an old, weather-beaten ghoul.

"Am I going blind?" the ghoul said raspily. "Or is that old Thoracks?"

Thoracks raised his blue paw.

"Evening, Orvis. Hope I didn't startle you."

The lanky ghoul scoffed.

"You know I don't spook easy."

The ghoul stood up with a creak and pop of bones. He was wearing snakeskin boots and a ten-gallon hat. His mottled skin was the texture of tough old rawhide. He looked like he'd been baked in an oven.

He came down the stairs slowly on his skinny legs and crossed the yard with a loping stride. Then he hooked his thumbs behind his belt buckle and stood there looking up at us with wizened hawk eyes.

"How you been, Thoracks?"

"Can't complain. Overworked, underpaid."

"Way of the world, I suppose," the ghoul said. He nodded towards me.

"What'd you bring me this time? A brunt or a clown?"

Clown?!

I thought he was teasing me. Then I looked down at my clothes...

I was still wearing my jester suit! It had been custom-made for me by the Queen's Royal Tailor. We'd left in such a hurry, I'd never had time to change out of it. Now it was smeared with seven shades of horse dung!

The ghoul twitched his half-eaten nose.

"Whatever he is, he reeks like a hog waller."

Thoracks chuckled awkwardly.

"Orvis, this is Spark. He, uh, had a little trouble at the Queen's Court recently. I had to get him out of there in a hurry. I figured there was no safer place to bring him than the Ghoul Ranch."

"Well, I reckon you're right about that," the old ghoul said. "We're so deep in the prairie, bad news can't even find us out here."

Let's hope so, I thought.

Thoracks socked me with his elbow.

"Spark, this is Orvis Pecadillo Rottenham. Folks around here call him Boss Rotten. He runs the Ghoul Ranch. He's been rustling cattle out here since I was just a little blue spud in nappies."

Boss Rotten tipped his ten-gallon hat towards me.

"Howdy," he said.

I nodded nervously.

"Uh...hi."

Thoracks eased the mule around.

"What do you think, Orvis? Got room for another ranch hand?"

Boss Rotten stroked his leathery cheek.

"Depends," he said. "Is he tough?"

Thoracks eyed me uncertainly.

"I'd say he's average...for a molly-coddled brunt."

Boss Rotten considered me for a moment.

"I reckon you can leave him. But just so you know, we're going to work him harder than a rented mule."

Thoracks lifted his head sagely.

"I'd expect nothing less," he said.

My stomach twisted into a knot.

Great...always more work!

Boss Rotten gestured with his stringy hand.

"Hop down and visit for a while. We'll have supper before long."

"Oh, I really can't," Thoracks said. "I was just giving Spark here a lift. I'll just water the mule, then I'm on my way."

"But you just got here!" Boss Rotten protested.

Thoracks bowed his horns.

"Duty calls, I'm afraid. Gotta head back to the office, make sure the place hasn't burnt to the ground yet."

Boss Rotten shrugged

"Have it your way then. Pull that cranky old mule to the trough and let him have a drink. He looks thirstier than a cockroach on a hot skillet."

Thoracks led the tired old mule to a trough and let him drink his fill. Then he steered the cart through the side yard and back onto the driveway. He stopped just long enough to pin me with a stern, yellow eye.

"Mind your manners, Spark. If I have to come back out here to pick you up, I'll be dragging you home behind the cart!"

My cheeks reddened a little.

"I'll do my best," I said begrudgingly.

Thoracks popped the reins. He and the mule passed beneath the bone-covered arch. I watched them vanish into the dark of the prairie. When their hoofbeats were gone, Boss Rotten and I faced each other.

He inspected me with a ranchman's eye.

"You look pretty thin in your britches, son," he said.

I wasn't too sure what that meant. But I got the idea.

"I've been better," I admitted.

Boss Rotten sighed.

"Welp, I've made ranch hands out of shabbier goods than you. We'll have to get you cleaned up eventually, I reckon. But first, you had better meet the other hands. Come on this way..."

He turned and stalked off on his lanky legs.

I went scampering after him.

4. Wet Behind the Ears

Boss Rotten led me towards the barn. It was a lofty, wooden husk of a building lit by hanging oil lamps. When we stepped inside, I saw that it was full of hay, old farm equipment, and ranch hands hard at work.

There was a young ghoul lady with curly red hair beneath her cowboy hat. She was coiling up what looked like a million feet of rope.

A square-jawed ogre in a bowler hat was shoveling dung.

Down at the far end, a huge, rocky-skinned troll in overalls was pounding horseshoes loudly on an anvil.

Cling, clang, blong!

Boss Rotten clapped his dry, scabby hands.

"Y'all hang it up for a second! We got company."

The three figures stopped what they were doing and dropped their ropes, shovels, and hammers. They came strolling forward slowly and stood there looking at me with their arms crossed.

Boss Rotten gave a jerk of his dusty head. "Everybody, this here is Spark. He's gonna be staying with us a while."

The square-jawed ogre snorted.

"Another lousy brunt? We just got rid of the last one!"

"Yeah," the young ghoul lady said. "It took forever to get the stain off the side of the barn. I've never seen a whale ox kick anyone that hard!"

"Y'all, hush!" Boss Rotten chided. "Thoracks just dropped him off. He's got to lay low for a while. So, I'm putting him to work. No use complaining about it."

The three of them groaned.

Boss Rotten turned to me.

"Spark, these are my ranch hands. Young ghoul lady there is Jolene. Ogre with the bad manners is Dewfus. And the big quiet fella is Cookie. Y'all say howdy."

"*Howdy*," they droned joylessly.

I was used to this sort of reception. Brunts were pretty much treated like rodents in Dungeonworld. I'd already made up my mind not to let it get to me, though.

Boss Rotten hocked something up and spat it into the dust.

"Anyways, that's enough lollygagging. Cookie, start rustling up some supper! Dewfus, finish slopping out the pens—"

"Shucks," Dewfus murmured. "Make the lousy brunt do it..."

Boss Rotten ignored him.

"Jolene, get this greenhorn cleaned up and fitted with a new pair of duds. We can't have him strutting around like a dung beetle from the circus. After that, show him around the Ghoul Ranch."

"If you say so, Boss," Jolene said.

She strolled forward and grabbed me by the shoulder. She had a strong grip for a decomposing ghoul!

"Come on, youngblood. You're getting the bucket treatment."

***

Jolene led me out behind the barn. There were a couple of decaying wooden stalls back here. She waved me towards one of them.

"Get inside and kick out of them duds," she said.

I did as I was told.

I slipped behind one of the wooden stalls and started shucking off my jester suit. It felt good to get out of that stinking getup! Afterward, I looked around the stall for soap, water, and sponges. But, I didn't see anything. Not even a crusty rag.

"Uh, do you have something I could wash up with?" I asked.

Jolene called back from outside.

"Sure, here you go..."

Her response came in the form of a cold bucket of water dumped over the top of the wooden stall. It splashed down over me like an icy wave! I couldn't hold back a shocked holler.

"Yowww!"

"Here's your scrubber," Jolene added.

A stiff bristly brush came lobbing over the wall of the stall. It clonked me on the head.

"Ouch!"

I stood there shivering, rubbing the back of my skull. I gazed at the huge brush on the ground. It looked like a porcupine on a stick. A grizzly bear could have scratched its back with this thing!

"I-is this all y-you h-have?" I asked, teeth chattering.

"If it's good enough for the hogs, it's good enough for the hands!" Jolene jeered.

I moaned.

I knew I wasn't getting clean any other way. So, I picked up the brush and began scrubbing my skin tenderly. It felt like I was washing with a spiny sea urchin! Meanwhile, I heard Jolene's boots wander off through the yard.

"I'm fetching you a set of clothes," she said. "If you need another cold bucket, the water trough is just outside."

By the time I'd managed to scrub off all the dung, I'd taken half my skin with it. My lips were blue, and my teeth hurt from chattering. I slipped out to dip another cold bucketful of water from the trough and used it to wash the rest of the filth away.

Eventually, Jolene came back whistling.

She flung a set of clothes over the stall wall.

"Here's your new duds," she said. "They belonged to a little goblin named Wilmer."

"What happened to Wilmer?" I asked.

"He got attacked by lava ants. Tough way to go. But I reckon his kit might fit a skinny little brunt like you."

I looked at the ragged pants and shirt.

They were covered with little pinpricks and bite marks!

Still, I was freezing in the wet stall with nothing but my pink, scuffed skin to keep me warm. So, I pulled on Wilmer's old jeans and shirt. Then I slid into the pair of leather boots Jolene slipped under the wall. I came out stomping my feet, trying to make the boots fit.

I raised my arms sheepishly.

"How do I look?"

Jolene lifted her sparse eyebrows.

"A sight better than you did," she said. "Heck, you might even be able to pass for a regular ranch hand before too long. I wouldn't hold my breath, though."

She spat into the dirt and turned around.

"Come on, youngblood. I'll show you how things work around here."

I kicked my feet into the boots once more. Then I set out across the yard behind Jolene's sauntering, plaid-shirted form.

5. Bone Chickens

JOLENE LED ME towards several large, dusty pastures and huts behind the barn. The air was full of clucking, mooing, and crowing. It smelled like musty animals back here.

Jolene waved a hand.

"This here's our livestock!" she said.

I looked at the animals milling about in the flickering torchlight. They definitely didn't look like the farm animals I was used to seeing in the human world. For one thing, they seemed too *big*.

"What is that?!" I asked.

A bull the size of a bus was stomping

around in a big pen with stone walls. His horns had to be ten feet across! His eyes were red, and muscles were standing out beneath his sleek fur.

"That's a whale ox!" Jolene said proudly.

"*A whale* ox?! I said. "Has it ever stomped anyone to death?"

"Not on purpose. Wanna pet him?"

I stared at the animal nervously.

"Umm..."

"He's sweeter than he looks. Watch."

She jumped onto the side of the pen and made kissy sounds.

The whale ox came thumping over.

I almost turned and ducked for cover!

"Here you go, baby," Jolene cooed.

She stuck her hand in her back pocket and pulled out a rotten carrot. She popped the carrot into her mouth and stuck her head into the pen.

The whale ox's huge tongue whipped out and took it straight from her lips!

"Good boy, Bubba!" she said.

She scratched his head while he munched the carrot. I stared at his seething red eye with wonder. He reminded me of a tank I'd seen in a museum once. But then again, tanks don't have massive horns!

"What do you do with a whale ox?" I asked.

"Cookie rides him when we're out rustling on the prairie," she said. "You can't put a troll on a normal horse. You'll just wind up with horse pudding."

"Makes sense," I told her.

She hopped down from the fence.

"Come on. More to see..."

We headed over to a little hut near the bullpen. Jolene flipped a latch on the wooden door, and we ducked into a room full of wire cages. There was a lot of squawking and clucking going on in here.

"This is the chicken coop," Jolene said.

I looked around at the cages.

"These are...*chickens?*" I asked.

"Sure, they are. Bone chickens!"

When she said bone chickens, she really meant *bone* chickens. There was nothing to them—just bones and a beak!

They were clucking around on little bony legs, shaking their rattling skulls and pecking through the hay.

Jolene plucked one from a wooden cage.

"Here, hold this," she said.

She shoved the chicken into my hands. I had no choice but to cradle it in my arms as she went rooting through the cage.

It felt like a twitchy bundle of sticks. I could see my hand on the other side of its rib cage!

"They don't seem to have a lot of meat on them," I said.

"You noticed?"

"How are you supposed to eat them?"

"You don't keep bone chickens to eat 'em," Jolene called, her head still lodged in the cage. "You keep them for their eggs...*bingo!*"

She pulled her hand out of the hay.

She was holding a big green egg. It was as shiny as a marble, and it seemed like it weighed a good amount. She put the egg into a little wicker basket next to the coop.

I couldn't believe it!

I held the chicken up and peered through its ivory ribcage.

"Uh...where do the eggs come from?"

Jolene rolled her eyes.

"Well, we don't bother asking them, do we? We just give them some privacy and let them do their business. Now hand her over!"

She took the bone chicken from my arms

"Back in you go, Bessie."

She popped the chicken back into the cage. Then she shooed me out of the chicken coop, closed the door behind us, and latched it. We continued right along.

"Those animals are all good and fine," Jolene said. "But, we keep our real pride and joy back here. The winged boars! Follow me..."

We walked up to a long split-rail fence and looked inside.

So, these are winged boars, I thought.

"Mmm," he grumbled.
"What's in the pot, Cook?" Jolene asked.
"Burgoo."
"Hoo-wee! My favorite!"

Jolene thumped me on the chest.

"Cookie whips up our slop around here," she said. "It's dang tasty! But be warned. Trolls have pebbles for taste buds. So, they like to make their dishes *extra* spicy."

I gave a tough shrug.

"I can take it," I said.

6. Rat Burgoo

JOLENE LED ME back to the stone farmhouse.

We walked through the back door and passed through a series of rooms that looked like they had been forgotten by time. They all had sagging floors, patchy furniture, and doors hanging off their hinges.

We found Cookie, the giant troll, in the kitchen.

He was hunched over a black metal stove, daintily tapping spices from a jar into a bubbling vat. He dipped one rocky finger into the contents of the vat, then popped it into his mouth and sucked on it.

Ghoul Ranch. We've got a thousand heads here, and more in the next pen yonder!"

I was mesmerized.

There was something sort of majestic about a pig with wings. I imagined myself rounding them up on horseback, a lasso twirling over my head. Real cowboy stuff. Suddenly, it seemed like this might not be such a bad place to work!

A loud bell clanged somewhere.

Cookie's deep, trollish voice called out.

"Supper's up!"

Jolene punched my arm.

"Come on, youngblood," she said. "Time for vittles!"

They were something to see! They looked like hairy, brown pigs with sharp tusks poking out their mouths. And sure enough, they had huge white wings sticking up from their backs!

They were running around the pen in big herds, their wings stretching and fanning gracefully. They stomped up a lot of dust as they ran, and the air was full of their oinking.

"Why don't they fly away?" I asked.

"We clip their wing muscles," Jolene said. "Right before they get too grown to head for the hills. Winged boars are our specialty at the

I'd eaten all sorts of weird stuff since I'd shown up in Dungeonworld, from moldy mushrooms to moose brains. I figured I could handle *anything* by now. But Jolene gave me a knowing smirk.

"We'll see about that," she said.

Boss Rotten and Dewfus, the ogre, came stomping into the kitchen. Boss Rotten gestured to an old wooden table with a flick of his hat.

"Everybody, park your paunches. Let's get some grub on the table!"

We sat down in wooden chairs around the table. Cookie came over, carrying the steaming vat by its handle. He plunked it down on a wooden trivet, and Jolene gave it a long, admiring whiff.

"Smells like a tip-top batch, Cookie!"

"I sure do love a nice, hot burgoo," Boss Rotten said with a wilting look. "Nobody whips it up better than our Cookie."

I watched smoke simmer off the top of the vat.

The bubbling liquid inside was a reddish-brown color. It was full of lumps and bumps. I definitely saw a full skeleton with a tail floating around on the surface. And there might have been some fur in there too.

"What's in it?" I asked.

"This here is *rat* burgoo," Boss Rotten said. "Cookie sure can dress up a rat. He stews 'em till their fur is just falling off. Then he rounds 'em out with some demon peppers, lava ant egg sacs, and heaps of maggoty corn!"

My stomach started to bubble just looking at it.

"And here come the fixin's!" Jolene said.

Cookie slid two more plates onto the table. One plate held a pile of crusty, black scorpions. The other plate held a wedge of cheese so green and stinky, it looked like it had just been dug up from the grave.

Boss Rotten winked at me.

"That there gorgonzola would strip the paint off a skunk!"

Good to know, I thought.

Cookie parked himself in a chair made of logs at the end of the table. Jolene clapped her hands.

"Let's eat, y'all!"

I prepared my stomach for all-out warfare.

Boss Rotten ladled huge dollops of rat burgoo into bowls and passed them around. Jolene carved slimy slices of green gorgonzola. Dewfus grabbed a handful of scorpions right off the plate and popped them into his mouth.

Crunch! Crunch! Crunch!

"Are those scorpions poisonous?" I asked him.

"Only for yellow-bellied brunts," he snarled.

I could already tell Dewfus didn't like me too much. That was fine—I didn't like him very much either. I grabbed a handful of scorpions and started wolfing them down like popcorn just to get his goat.

They were crispy!

I had to really chew up the hard pincers. And the pointy tails nearly poked holes in my throat! Still, I wouldn't give him the pleasure of seeing me squirm. I popped another handful right away.

Jolene slapped her knee.

"Yellow-bellied brunt my hindquarters," she said. "This boy's got rawhide for insides! Try that there burgoo, Spark."

I dipped my spoon into the brown rat burgoo and took a sip. I had to admit, it wasn't too bad for troll cooking. The rat meat was soft, and the stew was pleasantly tangy. I was just gulping down a second spoonful when the fire hit me...

"Holy guacamole!" I shouted.

It felt like I'd swallowed a hot poker!

My lips cracked and burned...

My tongue shriveled in my mouth...

Tears ran down my eyes...

"It's them lava ant egg sacs!" Boss Rotten

said. "Gets 'em every time."

Jolene held the cheese platter out to me.

"Here you go, Spark. Mellow it down with a little gorgonzola."

Normally, I wouldn't have laid a finger on that fart-smelling cheese. But I needed something to quench this burn! So, I pulled a slimy sliver off the tray, folded it in half, and poked it into my mouth.

Ugggh!

It tasted like dirty underwear smells!

I worked the greasy cheese between my teeth, trying not to puke. Eventually, the fiery burning in my mouth died down to a dull flame. But the juices in my stomach were boiling and bubbling.

I'll pay for this later, I thought.

"Welcome to life on the Ghoul Ranch!" Jolene said.

After supper was over, Boss Rotten threw down his napkin.

"Shoo! I'm fuller than a tick on a whale

ox's buttocks," he said. "I reckon we'd all better turn in early tonight. Big day tomorrow. Jolene, show this greenhorn to his sleeping quarters."

Jolene yanked me out of my chair.

"Come on, youngblood," she said.

I followed her, dripping sweat.

Jolene led me through the homestead with an oil lamp in her hand. We came to a little room in the back. Jolene pushed open the rope-and-wood door and pointed to a bed in the corner. It was just a metal cot with a hay-stuffed mattress on it.

"It ain't much," she said. "But it's better than sleeping on the floor."

"Fine by me," I told her.

I'd overdone it at dinner. My stomach felt like a smoking tar pit. I dragged myself across the room and plunked down onto the mattress. The bed squeaked like a rusty wheel.

"Rest up while you can," Jolene said. "We'll most likely work you to death tomorrow. Oh, and by the way...the privy is down the hall."

"The what?"

"The bathroom," she said. "That rat burgoo won't sit still till morning."

I groaned again.

My insides were simmering like a hot cauldron. But I was too drowsy to worry much about it now. I swung my legs up onto the bed and fell asleep with my boots on.

7. Spooky

I ROLLED AROUND ON my mattress all night in a hot sweat.

Jolene was right. I sprang up more than once that night to rush to the privy down the hall! Each time, I came staggering back, woozy and frazzled. I drifted in and out of sleep, wondering when it would all end.

Eventually, a bone rooster crowed outside.

Jolene burst through my door.

"Rise and shine, youngblood! It's rustlin' time!"

I rolled over, hands on my stomach.

"I might need a sick day, Jolene. I've got

burgoo belly."

She wasn't having it, though.

"Nonsense! No days off at the ranch. Come on, lazybones!"

She stomped across the room, grabbed my bootheels, and yanked me out of bed. I landed flat on the floor with a *thud!*

She was already rumbling through the door.

"Meet me out by the corral!"

I got up, sweaty and wobbly, and followed her.

Outside the farmhouse, Dewfus, Cookie, and Boss Rotten were waiting with cups of coffee in their hands. When they saw me coming, big smiles crossed their ugly faces. They looked like they were ready for some entertainment.

"What's so funny?" I said irritably.

"We're makin' a real cowboy out of you today," Boss Rotten said.

"Oh yeah? How?"

"We're pickin' you out a horse!"

He led me over to a large pen beside the hog corral. Here, a bunch of sickly-looking horses was cantering around, neighing and snorting. Leathery skin showed through their patchy fur. Their hip bones jutted out like knobs.

Ghoul horses, I thought.

I had seen ghoul horses before. They look like zombie versions of real horses. But these seemed crazier than the ones I'd run across. They kept tossing their heads, leaping into the air, and kicking up their heels.

"What's wrong with them?" I asked. "They look totally wild."

"That's because they *are* wild," Jolene replied. "We plucked 'em straight off the prairie. They ain't never been ridden before. You have to *break 'em*—get 'em used to the saddle. That's your job today."

I looked at the feral beasts.

"You want me to ride one of these things?!"

"It's tradition on the Ghoul Ranch," Boss Rotten said. "You can't work a ranch without a horse. And you can't ride a horse you ain't broken yourself."

A pack of the ghoul horses came rumbling by the fence. Their huge hooves clobbered the ground.

Whop-whop-whop!

They smelled like raw death!

I immediately wanted out of this whole thing.

"I don't know," I said, shaking my head.

Dewfus snorted.

"What'd I tell you? I knew a yellow-bellied brunt couldn't break no wild ghoul horse. He ain't got the guts for it!"

My jaw clenched tight.
Something hot bubbled up inside me...
And it wasn't rat burgoo!
See, I can't stand being called *chicken*. Even back in the human world, I was constantly taking stupid risks and dares just to prove a point. If someone says I can't do something, I have to do it...
Especially if that someone is a dim-witted ogre!
I looked Dewfus in his beady eyes.

"Show me to the horse," I said.

Jolene whooped.

"Get ready, youngblood. We've got just the one for you!"

Jolene led me to a smaller pen near the chicken coop. Here, one skinny ghoul horse had been separated from the others.

Even by ghoul horse standards, this one looked pretty sickly. He was chestnut brown, with ribs showing through his flanks. As we approached the pen, he skittered and stamped wildly.

Jolene ducked through the fence.

I had no choice but to climb in after her.

"We call him Spooky," Jolene said, walking up to the horse. "Because he's scared of dang near everything. You ever been on a ghoul horse?"

"Just once," I replied.

I had made a headlong dash on a ghoul horse once on my way to join the Dungeonworld Army. But I had been riding doubles with a ghoul named Putrilda that time. I wasn't too sure how I'd handle one by myself.

I didn't have time to question it, though. Before I knew what was happening, Jolene hooked her bony hands under my arms and lifted me off the ground.

"You shouldn't have a problem then!" she said.

She heaved me straight onto Spooky's back.

Right away, he freaked out.

Naaayyy!

Spooky reeled onto his hind legs, hooves kicking the air. I lost my grip and went flying!

Whump!

I landed on my butt in the dirt.

"Nunchucks!" I shouted.

Boss Rotten and Dewfus just about died laughing. Even Cookie was doubled over barking out troll guffaws—he sounded like an enormous, croaking bullfrog.

"HAR-HAR-HAR!"

I got up, red-faced, rubbing my bruised rear end. Jolene had tears of mirth on her green, rotten cheeks. She was clutching her sides.

"You gotta hold on tighter than that, youngblood!"

"I wasn't ready!" I growled back.

She grabbed my shoulder.

"Come on," she said. "Let's try her again."

I swatted her scabby hands away.

"No!" I said. "I'll do it myself!"

Jolene stepped back, wheezing. They all seemed to think this was a real lark. A fun game of "Pick On The New Brunt." I clenched my jaw.

We'll see about this...

I crept up to Spooky and stroked his side.

"Easy, boy," I said. "Take it easy."

Very gently, I grabbed the saddle. I slid my boot into the stirrup.

Spooky grunted.

I knew I was only going to have one shot at this. All the others were watching intently. So, I took a deep breath and calmed my nerves. With a burst of energy, I leaped onto Spooky's back.

NAAAYYY!

Spooky reared up like a jack-in-the-box.

But this time, I held on! I grabbed the pommel with one hand and threw the other hand into the air. I rode him like a real cowboy, whooping and hollering for everything I was worth!

8. Bronc Rider

SPOOKY STAMPED AND snorted...
He backed and reared...
He kicked his heels up like he was trying to punch a hole in the sky.

I whipped and see-sawed with him through every turn. We must have spun a hundred circles. I thought I would puke! Just when I felt like I couldn't hold on a second longer, I yanked the reins as hard as I could.

"Knock it off!" I shouted.

To my amazement, Spooky listened.

He came to a dead standstill in the center of the pen and stood looking around like he'd just snapped out of a trance. He shook his head, snorting into the dirt.

I saw my chance to calm him down.

"Th-that's right, boy," I said queasily. "Easy does it..."

I patted his neck a little bit.

Spooky whinnied and knickered.

I carefully gathered the reins and gave them a gentle pop. Spooky danced around on his hooves a bit. Then he began trotting around the pen in a slow circle.

The other ranch hands watched me with their jaws hanging wide open. As I came by the fence, Boss Rotten yanked off his hat and slapped it on the ground.

"I'll be darned!" he shouted

"Look at that!" Jolene said.

"Whoo-eee!" Cookie howled.

I trotted Spooky around as they cheered and hollered. The only person who didn't seem thrilled about it was Dewfus. He just pulled his bowler hat low and sulked.

"Not bad for a lousy brunt," he muttered.

I didn't care. I was over the moon!

I took Spooky for a few more turns around the pen. Then I brought him once more to the fence and slid out of the saddle like a cowboy. Jolene stepped in and took the reins.

"Well done, youngblood!" she said. "You're a natural bronc rider!"

"Thanks!" I replied, dizzy but happy.

I climbed out of the pen, feeling like a hero.

Boss Rotten slapped me hard on the back. Then he put a stringy hand on my shoulder and started guiding me away from the corral.

"There's more to you than I thought, greenhorn," he said. "Come on, I'm taking you under my wing today!"

He called back over his shoulder.

"Cookie, take Bubba out riding. Dewfus, muck the dung out of his pen."

"Dangit!" Dewfus shouted.

I threw a nasty grin back at him.

What a great start to the day!

For the next several hours, I walked all over the Ghoul Ranch with Boss Rotten. He told me old rancher stories about all the things he'd seen: droughts, stampedes, crazy horses. He was good company!

"Yep, I've been raising livestock since prairie dust was young," Boss Rotten said. "And I'll tell you what, greenhorn. There ain't no finer occupation for a ghoul. Why, it suits me right down to my toenails!"

I looked at his feet…

His yellow

toenails were actually poking through his ratty boots!

This could have grossed me out. But you get used to these things when you hang around with ghouls. I decided just to brush it off.

"Yessir," Boss Rotten continued. "I like to be out here where the air is fresh and the breeze is fine. Just take a big old sniff."

He drew a fluttering, wheezing breath.

I took a deep breath as well.

It smelled like pig poop and dirt out here. But even that was an improvement from how Dungeonworld usually smelled—like sweaty monsters and mildew. So, I let out a contented sigh.

"Come on," Boss Rotten said. "Let's amble over to the hog pen."

We walked around the bone chicken hut to the winged boar corral. Boss Rotten and I propped our boots on the bottom rail and hooked our elbows over the top. We looked out at the stamping, snorting boars.

"Have you ever seen a finer mess of hogs?" Boss Rotten asked.

"Nope, I haven't," I said.

This was totally true.

Until yesterday, I had never seen a boar in my life!

"Winged boars is what makes the Ghoul Ranch go 'round, greenhorn," he said. "Every ranch hand has to get a feel for them. You know how you do that?"

"No," I said. "How?"

"You got to get right in there with them."

Boss Rotten pulled his boot down from the fence.

"Come on," he said. "It's time for you to meet the herd."

Before I could protest, he grabbed me by the shoulder and shoved me forward. I tumbled through the fence rails headfirst. Boss Rotten folded his lanky frame and ducked in behind me.

Just like that, I was among the winged boars!

9. Herd Mentality

RIGHT AWAY, I knew I was in over my head.

The huge hogs stamped and skittered around us. Their trampling hooves pounded up dust. Their sharp tusks flashed by like white knives. I was worried one of them might gore me!

Boss Rotten slapped them with his hat.

"Woah now, piggies!" he

called. "Make room!"

"What exactly are we doing in here?" I said.

"I told you...getting a feel for the hogs!"

"Yeah, but what does that mean?!"

"It means you've got to get on their level," he said. "Just become one with the herd. You can't raise a hog if you can't *think* like a hog!"

But I don't want to think like a hog! I thought.

Boss Rotten didn't seem to care about my particular feelings, though. He began carving a path through the herd.

"Woah now, piggies! Woah now!"

I tried to follow along behind him as quickly as possible. But I couldn't make any headway through the musty, sweaty mob. It was like hanging around a bunch of fat, hairy geese. Their flapping wings were beating me to death!

"Oof! Ouch! Ow!"

I threw my hands over my head and cowered.

Pigs boxed me around from every angle.

I got battered by butts. Smacked by wings. Several tried to kick me into the air like a soccer ball. I felt like I was in a pork pinball machine!

"Hey, wait up," I cried. "I need a little help here!"

"Don't be shy now, greenhorn," Boss Rotten called. "Show 'em who's the boss hog!"

I watched his tall, stick-like figure and enormous hat wade through the swarming mass of bodies. He looked like a broom bobbing in a hairy, feathery sea.

Suddenly, I was on my own.

A whole new wave of hog bodies started buffeting me from both sides. I was getting squeezed between hindquarters. *This would be a terrible way to die,* I thought. *Squished by hog butts!*

I decided to quit playing nice.

"Knock it off, you hairy pork chops!" I shouted.

I started throwing my weight around. I thrashed and kicked as hard as I could. I began elbowing and shoving hogs aside.

"Get your fat booties off me!" I wailed.

For a moment, it seemed to work.

The slightest bit of space opened up around me.

That's the ticket! I thought.

I kept shoving my way through the herd, feeling tougher by the minute. But I might have shoved a little too hard. One of the biggest boars spun around with an angry squeal and glared at me with enraged pig eyes.

I stood my ground.

"What are you looking at?" I said.

The hog answered by pawing the dirt viciously with its hoof. I suddenly realized that its tusks were each a foot long and razor-sharp. A ridge of dark, spiky hair stood up on its back.

It lowered its brawny head to the ground.

SQUEEEAAAL!

The hog bolted straight for me!

"Oh crud," I mumbled.

I did the only thing any self-respecting brunt would do...

I ran like a coward!

"AAAGGGHHHH!"

The Ghoul Ranch

I spun around and dashed off so fast I left a Spark-shaped hole in the dust cloud behind me. My boots slipped and slid as I went sprinting through the corral, dodging hogs left and right.

"Get out of the way, you stupid pigs!" I screamed.

Hairy bodies scattered from our path. The pigs at least had the sense to clear a lane for me as the huge boar continued its charge. I could hear its hooves stomping the ground behind me.

Wha-whump! Wha-whump! Wha-whump!

My mind was racing.

The boar was almost on top of me.

I could feel its steamy breath on my back!

I'm doomed!

That's when I saw the fence up ahead…

It was only twenty feet away.

My boots were barely underneath me. My arms were spinning like a windmill. With every ounce of energy I had left, I dove headfirst through the fence rails and went tumbling onto the hard prairie dirt outside.

SQUUEEEAAAL!

The boar came to a screeching stop behind me. Dust sprayed from beneath its chunky hooves.

The boar glared at me through the fence, flapping its huge wings menacingly. It reared up on its hind legs once. Then, with an angry snort, it turned and went trotting back into the herd.

"That's r-right," I said shakily. "R-run away…"

I got up and dusted myself off.

I couldn't believe I was still in one piece!

Somewhere in the distance, I could hear

Boss Rotten still in the corral. He was shouting, "Woah, piggies! Woah!" I wasn't sure how I was supposed to find him again without getting killed.

Forget it, I thought. *I've had enough winged boars for one day.*

I decided just to go back to the farmhouse.

I turned around and was about to stalk off when something unusual caught my eye. I peered out into the darkness of the prairie. Several yards away, I saw what looked like a little pink ball hopping around on the ground.

I walked several steps towards it.

The little pink ball turned into a chubby, prancing body.

I couldn't believe my eyes...

It was a teeny, tiny winged boar!

It was chasing a tarantula across the ground, squealing with delight. Every few feet, it would leap into the air, hover for a few seconds on fluttering wings, then plummet back to the ground.

I laughed in amazement.

"Hey there, little guy!" I said. "Did you

get lost?"

Oink, oink!

I scooped the pig up and inspected it. It was a boy pig. He had tiny tusks and an unusually large pig snout. When he looked up at me with his little blue eyes, I could have sworn he smiled.

You must have just slipped out of the pen! I thought.

I tucked him into the crook of my arm. "Come on," I said. "I can't leave you out here all by yourself."

    I walked off, carrying him like a little pink football.

10. One Little Winglet

When I made it back to the front of the corral, Boss Rotten had just emerged through the fence. He was slapping dust off of himself with his hat.

"Who-eee!" he said. "Them hogs are rowdy today."

He spied the little bundle in my arms.

"Whatcha got there, greenhorn?"

"I don't know," I said. "I just found him."

I showed him the little boar.

His weepy, yellow eyes lit up.

"It's a *winglet!*" he said.

"A winglet?"

"Sure! A baby hog!" Boss Rotten said.

"This one's out of season, though. They mostly don't show up till springtime."

I bounced the little winglet in my arms.

"So, this one's special?" I asked.

"Dang right he is! Come on, let's show the gang!"

We walked back to the farmhouse to find Jolene and Dewfus pitchforking a huge mound of hay. Jolene was rolling up her sleeves. Boss Rotten slapped me on the back as we approached.

"Look what old Spark found!" he called.

I held the little winglet up for the others to see.

Jolene pushed her hat back.

"I'll be danged!" she said. "A stray winglet!"

Even Dewfus seemed interested. His greasy brow crumpled up.

"Where'd you find it?" he grunted.

I told them about how I'd spotted the little guy prancing and fluttering around on the edge of the prairie. Even as I talked, his little hummingbird wings started to whir. He nearly rose out of my arms.

"Looky that!" Jolene said. "He's just about taken flight!"

Boss Rotten chuckled happily again.

"That was a heck of a find, greenhorn. He's just a few days away from flying. In no time at all, he'd have wandered off and made for the hills. We'd never see him again."

I looked up, surprised.

"Could he really survive on his own out there?" I asked.

"Oh sure," Boss Rotten said. "Winged boars are hardy. He would've just flapped off and found himself a new home somewhere else."

"Nabbed him just in time!" Dewfus said. He laughed deviously.

I eyed him sideways.

"What should we do with him?" I asked.

"Well, you can keep an eye on him tonight," Boss Rotten said. "Then, tomorrow morning, we'll clip his wings and tuck him back in with the herd."

Something in my heart went cold.

"Clip his wings?" I said. "What for?"

Boss Rotten gave me a gap-toothed smile.

"Why, so he doesn't fly off and head for the hills! A winglet like that will turn into a good-sized hog. Heck, he'll probably fetch a thousand doinks at the meat market!"

"Make us a nice fine profit!" Dewfus said.

The cold spot in my heart turned to ice.

"B-but...we can't sell him," I said.

"Why not?" Boss Rotten asked.

I looked at the sweet bundle in my hands.

I searched for a good reason.

"Because...I *like* him," I said.

Boss Rotten, Dewfus, and Jolene looked at me blankly for a moment. Then they burst into uproarious laughter. Jolene staggered sideways onto Dewfus's shoulder. It was like I'd told a real gut-buster!

"Hogs ain't pets, you crazy brunt!" Dewfus said. "They're meat! That's what we raise 'em for!"

Jolene gave me a consoling pat on the back.

"He's right, youngblood," she said. "We raise hogs to send 'em to market. That's what all this fuss is about. Just the same, you done a good job nabbing this one before he wandered off. A heck of a catch!"

The dinner bell suddenly clanged.

"Supper's up!" Cookie called.

Boss Rotten slapped his hat on his leg.

"Come on, y'all," he said. "Let's get us some grub."

I carried the winglet up the stairs behind the laughing crowd. Every step I took was like a funeral trudge.

11. The Meat Market

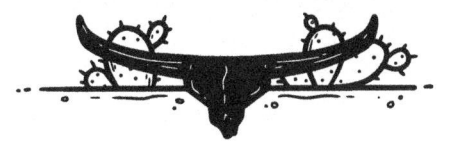

COOKIE HAD WHIPPED up a killer supper that night: hot tamales, lizard skewers, and grasshopper popcorn. Everyone dug in. But I could hardly bring myself to eat more than a few grasshoppers.

"What's the matter, Spark?" Jolene asked. "You ain't touched your lizards."

I cast around for an excuse.

"Uhh…stomach's a little upset," I said lamely.

Dewfus shrugged.

"More for me!"

He snatched the sauce-covered lizards off my plate and sucked them right off the skewer with a loud *slurp!*

I pushed my chair out and stood up.

"I'm feeling pretty sleepy," I said. "I might head to bed."

Boss Rotten watched me with a strange gleam in his eye.

"All right, greenhorn. Don't let the bed bugs bite."

"I won't..."

I picked the little winglet up off the floor beside me.

Tucking him under my arm, I headed down the hall to my bedroom.

In my room, I paced around anxiously, wringing my hands. I had no idea what to do.

You should have known this was coming, I thought. *I mean, you don't raise hogs for nothing. People eat them!*

Somehow, I had managed to ignore that fact. Now, as I watched the tiny winglet flutter around the room like a little balloon, I couldn't seem to think of anything else. He was so innocent and sweet!

"Just relax," I told myself. "Everything will work out fine."

But how, my mind screamed.

The walls had no answer.

I stalked around the room until my head hurt from worrying. Eventually, I got tired and sat down on my lumpy bed. The mattress springs groaned beneath me.

I eased back with my boots on and stared at the ceiling. I tried closing my eyes, desperately hoping for sleep to come. But I kept seeing the little winglet hog-tied with an apple in his mouth!

Cripes!

When too many sleepless hours had passed, I sat up and looked around the dark room. The little winglet was curled up on the floor like a pink potato. His feathery wings were pressed tightly to his back. He was snoring away happily.

I watched him with dread in my stomach.

I can't let anything happen to him, I thought.

I needed to find a way out. *But how?!*

I considered the situation for a while.

A desperate decision came to me...

I'll just let him go, I thought. *I'll take him out onto the prairie somewhere and turn him loose. In the morning, I'll say that I left the door open by accident, and he just ran off. How mad can they get about one little pig?*

It might not have been a very good idea. But I didn't have a better one at the moment. So, I decided to go with it.

I got up off my cot with a creak.

"Hey, buddy," I hissed. "*Wake up*."

The winglet came awake with a snuffle. He looked at me sleepily.

Oink?

"We have to go somewhere," I told him.

Oink, oink?

I picked him up and tucked him under my arm.

"Just stay quiet for a second, okay?"

Very carefully, I tiptoed over to the door and listened. I thought Dewfus and Cookie would have been snoring like chainsaws by now. But the farmhouse was completely quiet. The place was as still as a grave.

The winglet started to yawn.

"Quiet!" I hissed.

I clapped a hand over his snout.

My heart was pounding in my chest.

I pulled open my door and went sneaking through the house silently. At the back door, I gave one more look around the house and then vanished into the smoky night air.

I went stealing through the dusty yard like a phantom. Every scratch and skitter of creatures in the dark made my heart leap. I must have been squeezing the winglet too tightly because he let out a mild squeal.

Oiiink!

"Shhhh!" I hissed. "Don't make a sound..."

We slipped into the barn. It was pitch black in here. I hadn't brought a torch, and I couldn't see anything. I cupped my free hand over my mouth.

"Spooky!" I whispered. "Spooky, where are you?"

I heard a whinny at the back of the barn.

I went creeping in that direction...

I found Spooky munching hay near the saddle rack. His patchy tail was swishing. I petted him a little to calm him down.

"Don't worry, Spooky," I said. "We're just going out riding."

Really, I was the nervous one.

I didn't know what I was doing!

I only knew one thing—there was no way I would let the winglet get sold at the meat market. Not today, not tomorrow, not ever!

I set him down on the ground for a moment. Then I pulled a small saddle down from the wall and put it on Spooky's back.

Spooky groaned nervously.

"Easy, buddy," I said. "Nothing to fear."

It took me a while to get the saddle and reins adjusted. I wasn't sure I'd done it right, but I scooped up the winglet and climbed onto Spooky's back anyways. I took the reins in my free hand and steered us away from the saddle rack.

"All right, you two. Let's take it nice and easy..."

I was just starting to trot us through the dark room to the big barn door on the far end when, suddenly, a match flared in the darkness.

Boss Rotten held it up at eye level.
"Where do you think you're goin'?" he said.

12. Hog Thief

MY HEART LEAPED into my throat.

The ghoul ranchman didn't look happy. He used the match to light an oil lamp. The bright light revealed that others were with him. Cookie was standing in the way of the barn door. Jolene hung beside him, watching me with a glum expression.

I brought Spooky to a halt.

"Me?" I said casually. "I was just... heading out for a ride."

Boss Rotten stroked his dusty cheek.

"That's funny. I thought you were going to bed early."

I gulped.

"Changed my mind, I guess…"

His eye roamed to the little winglet on my saddle.

"You wasn't thinking of running off with that pig, was you?" he asked.

The look on his face told me everything.

The game was up.

I spoke with a quavering voice.

"I'm not letting you send him off to the market," I said. "He's my friend, and you don't let your friends get eaten. I'm setting him free."

Boss Rotten laughed mirthlessly.

"Well then, that makes you no better than a dang *hog thief!* And we don't take kindly to hog thieves around here."

He tipped his chin.

"Cookie…Jolene…go grab that hog."

Cookie lumbered forward obediently.

Jolene followed with a rope in her hands.

"Now, just stay put, youngblood," she said. "We don't want to hurt you."

I don't want you to hurt me either! I thought.

That only left one option…

SCRAM!

I spun Spooky around and began trotting him towards the door at the other end of the barn. I was almost there when Boss Rotten called out behind me.

"Dewfus, stop him!"

The door ahead of me swung open…

Dewfus was standing there. He had his strong hands spread wide like a wrestler. He looked like he was ready to tackle me and beat me to a pulp!

I made a split-second decision.

"Spooky," I shouted. "*Trample!*"

Spooky whinnied wildly, his front hooves kicking the air. Then he charged forward in a sudden gallop. We barreled right over Dewfus like he was an ogre-shaped speed bump.

"OOOF!"

I ducked my head as we dashed through the doorway.

With that, we were out in the open air...

And I was heading for the horizon!

"Get that brunt!" Boss Rotten shouted behind me.

I didn't slow down to look back, though. I went tearing off into the Dungeonworld night with the little winglet bouncing on the saddle in front of me. Spooky was still neighing loudly and tossing his head.

I didn't have a plan.

I didn't even have a destination!

I just knew that I had to get as far away from the Ghoul Ranch as possible. So, I swung us to the right and began heading for the nearby mesas and canyons. I figured I could lose them somewhere in the maze of hills.

We just need a little bit of a head start, I thought.

But I could already hear ghoul horses whinnying and a whale ox braying behind me. I heard Boss Rotten's voice calling, "Yahh! Yahh! Hurry up, get that brunt!"

This was going to be an old-fashioned horse race.

And I was the slowest cowboy out here...

13. On the Run

WE DASHED MADLY through the darkened prairie.

By now, Spooky knew that something was wrong. He was running with wild, fearful abandon. But the winglet didn't have a care in the world. He balanced himself on the saddle, wiggling and squealing with joy.

Oiiink! Oiiink!

"Sit still!" I told him. "You're going to fall off!"

I suddenly felt very foolish.

Here I was risking my neck for a pig I had just met. And I still didn't even know where I was going! There was no time for second thoughts, though. The only thing left to do was *run.*

I turned once in the saddle to look behind us.

I saw pinpricks of light glowing out on the prairie. Torches flickering in the dark. I could hear the sound of ghoulish voices howling.

"Keep on 'em, gang! Run that lousy hog thief down!"

Great, I thought. *They're gaining on us!*

"Come on, Spooky!" I said. "Turn on the turbo boosters!"

But poor Spooky seemed to be maxed out. He was already sweating up a storm. I was afraid if I pushed him any harder, he might just collapse.

Grim reality began to dawn on me.

We're not going to make it, I thought.

I almost gave in to despair.

But just then, I noticed a line out on the horizon. I studied it in the dark and quickly realized what it was...

A cliff!

We were racing towards the edge of a

steep canyon! It seemed to stretch for miles to our left and right. I could already see the drop-off and all the wide-open air beyond the ledge.

This might have seemed like the end of the line.

But I suddenly had an idea.

"Hold on!" I told the little winglet.

Shaking the reins, I hunkered down in the saddle like a jockey. I pushed Spooky onward as hard as I dared. We went pounding straight towards the dangerous cliff…

We were just yards from the ledge when I finally pulled up on the reins.

"WOOOAH, BOY!"

Spooky came to a skidding halt.

He sent a wave of rocks cascading over the edge.

KSSSHHH!

I didn't waste a second…

I grabbed the winglet and hopped down from the saddle. Holding him in my arms, I went running towards the lip of the canyon. I stopped at the edge and cautiously craned my neck to look over the precipice.

It was a two-hundred-foot drop, straight down!

This will work, I thought grimly.

I held up the winglet so we were eye-to-eye.

"Look, buddy," I said. "There's only one way out of this…you have to *fly*. I can't get away from them. But *you can*. They won't be able to catch you if you fly away!"

He smiled at me with his little blue eyes.

He didn't understand a word I was saying.

"Don't you get it?" I shouted. "When they catch us, they're going to clip your wings. They'll send you off to the meat market, and somebody will eat you! You have to escape while you can!"

He squirmed and wriggled. He thought I was playing with him.

I have to get this through his head! I thought.

As far as I could see, there was only one way to do that. Gripping him with both hands, I held him out over the ledge...

Right away, he panicked!

Oiiink! Oiiink!

His little hooves backpedaled in the air. He squealed and writhed in my hands. His wings fluttered pitifully. I reeled him back in and gazed at him once more.

"You...have...to...*fly!*" I told him. "There's no other way out!"

Fear flashed in his pig eyes.

I thought he understood me now. But he

looked overwhelmed with terror. It seemed like the last thing he wanted was to jump into that canyon.

"You can do it," I assured him. "I've watched you flapping around all day. You're ready to fly, I know you are! You just have to believe in yourself!"

But whether I was right or wrong, it was suddenly too late. Hooves thundered and rumbled nearby.

Boss Rotten's gang had finally caught up to us.

They came riding up out of the darkness, whooping and hollering. Their torches swung as they reined in their horses just paces away from us. Boss Rotten's face was pinched in an angry scowl.

"You got nowhere left to run, green horn!" he said.

I looked at the canyon drop-off.

I looked back at the posse.

"I guess I don't," I admitted.

Boss Rotten sucked on his moldy teeth and spat into the dirt.

"Just bring me that hog," he said. "And I might let you leave here in one piece."

I cradled the little winglet innocently.

"What hog?" I asked. "This one?"

Boss Rotten narrowed his eyes.

"You heard me. Bring him over here."

I acted like I was considering it for a moment.

Then I shrugged.

"I've got a better idea. How about you go bury your head in dung."

Boss Rotten's dry scabby face crinkled with rage.

"Someone go fetch that hog!" he roared.

Dewfus slid down from his saddle. I could see a fresh bump on his forehead where Spooky had used him as a doormat. My heart was beating in my chest as he came striding over.

It's now or never, I thought.

I turned around to face the cliff.

"If you want this hog," I said, "you can catch him yourself!"

I held the winglet up like the world's fattest paper airplane. His soft, pink belly was resting on my palm. I muttered a quick prayer to the patron saint of flying pigs. Then, mustering all my strength, I drew back my arm and launched him into the void.

"Fly, buddy, fly!" I shouted.

I counted heartbeats as the winglet sailed through the air. He looked like a perfect pork missile!

His hooves were sprawled. His ears were flattened. His snout was pointing straight forward, and his wings were angled back. He flew a good ten feet out into the open air.

Then, he began to plummet...

I gasped.

"Nooo!"

He turned nose-down and began bombing towards the canyon floor below. Sweat poured down my forehead as I watched him sink. He was going to hit the dirt like a fuzzy lawn dart!

I've killed him! I thought.

But just when I was sure all hope was lost, something amazing happened.

He spread his wings.

14. Hog Tied

His feathers caught the air like parachutes.

Whooosh.

He came swooping out his dive like a fighter pilot. In one long, graceful motion, he went careening out over the canyon floor below, smooth as a seagull.

He let out a triumphant call as he flew.

Oiiiink!

I punched the air.

"Way to go, buddy!"

I watched as he soared upward on a warm, desert draft. He wheeled around, his blue eyes flashing out of the darkness. I could see a radiant smile on his pig lips. Then, as the wind shifted, he turned once more and began flying out over the open land beyond.

Soon, he was just a pink dot in the darkness.

I had to choke back a tear.

He's gone, I thought.

But I knew he was free. And now that he

could fly, I figured he always would be.

Unfortunately, I couldn't say the same for myself.

I turned around to see the whole gang waiting behind me. They looked pretty unhappy, to say the least.

Boss Rotten was uncoiling his lasso in his ropy hands. Dewfus was cracking his knuckles.

"I bet you think you're some kind of hero," Boss Rotten said.

I shrugged defiantly.

"The pig is safe," I told him. "That's all I care about."

"Right noble of you, greenhorn."

He gave another jerk of his head.

"Dewfus...*nab him*."

Dewfus strode forward.

With his green, thorny hands, he snatched me straight off my feet. For a moment, I thought he would chuck me into the canyon! But instead, he tossed me to the ground and pulled my hands behind my back.

Boss Rotten threw him a rope.

"Tie him up," he said. "And don't be tender with the knots. Jolene, you ride on back and send for Thoracks. We're shipping this hog thief back to where he came from."

My cocky confidence abandoned me.

I swallowed.

"Does this mean I'm fired?" I asked.

Dewfus hog-tied my hands and feet together behind me. I felt like a thanksgiving turkey!

For the ride back to the Ghoul Ranch, they put me on the rear end of Cookie's rumbling whale ox. This meant that I had a troll butt *and* whale ox butt in my face. *Totally disgusting!*

When we finally made it back to the ranch, Dewfus tossed me head-first into the barn like a sack of potatoes. I lay there, spitting out hay.

"Don't go nowhere!" Dewfus snarled.

"Oh, right," I said. "I was just about to dash off!"

He slammed the barn door shut.

I've been in some tight spots in Dungeonworld. I've learned that, when things can't get any worse, it's best to just get some sleep. But let me tell you—it's hard to relax when you're curled up like a banana!

The only thing that made it tolerable was the memory of the winglet soaring like a plane. I could still see his blue, happy eyes flashing at me out of the darkness. It made me feel like I was soaring up there with him…rather than lying here next to horse turds.

I must have fallen asleep eventually, because I awoke to a bucket of cold water splashed in my face.

"Rise and shine, youngblood."

I looked up to find Jolene standing above me. Thoracks was standing next to her. He had a look of disappointment on his blue, bullish face. But hey, what else is new?

Boss Rotten wandered up next to him.

"There lies your hog thief," he said.

Thoracks sighed.

"I'm sorry about this, Orvis. I'll pay for the missing hog."

"Don't bother! Just find yourself a hole somewhere and drop this yellow-bellied lizard down it. And don't bring me no more brunts!"

"Fair enough," Thoracks agreed.

He picked me up like a piece of luggage. My bones popped, and my muscles screamed!

He carried me over to the same old wheezy mule and cart we'd ridden in on. Without much ceremony, he tossed me into the back. I discovered, gratefully, that he'd at least shoveled out the dung this time!

Thoracks climbed into the front. He sat there on the bench, guiltily searching for words.

"Eh, I reckon I'll see you later?" he said.

Boss Rotten scoffed.

"Don't make it too soon!"

Thoracks nodded sadly and popped the reins.

As the mule started forward, I gazed back at the four members of the Ghoul Ranch. They were all watching me go with angry frowns. Boss Rotten's weathered old mug was puckered up like he'd bitten into a lemon.

Oh well, I thought. *Another day, another job...*

Soon, it was just the two of us out on

the dark prairie. We rode along in silence for a while. I kept trying to think of something I could say to make things better. But before I could puzzle it out, Thoracks broke the ice.

"So, you threw a pig off a cliff, huh?"

I piped up to defend myself.

"They were going to send him off to market! Someone was going to eat him!"

"That's generally what happens to hogs," Thoracks replied.

"I know," I said. "But I couldn't let it happen...not to that one."

I expected a furious outburst.

A volcanic tirade.

Instead, Thoracks sighed.

"I reckon I can't blame you," he said.

I arched my neck to look at him.

"Wait...really?"

"Yeah. That's why I never made it as a cowboy myself. Just didn't have the heart for it, I suppose."

My whole outlook changed.

I suddenly felt relieved!

I twisted uncomfortably on the wagon floor.

"Great!" I said. "So, uh...do you want to untie me now?"

Thoracks shook his horned head dreamily.

"Not just yet," he replied.

My brow creased.

I wriggled in my knots.

"Thoracks, come on...I'm dying here."

He shrugged.

"Tough break, kid."

I scoffed indignantly.

I can't believe this!

"If you don't untie me," I said, "I'll just blabber the whole way back. You won't get a moment of peace and quiet! I'll talk and talk and talk...is that what you really want?"

This seemed like a pretty good argument to me. But Thoracks raised a blue, clawed finger.

"Actually, I brought something for that."

I screwed my face up.

"Really? What is it?"

He reached into a sack beside him and pulled something out.

He held it up...

It was a shiny, red apple.
"*This*," he said.

I squinted in confusion.
"An apple?" I said. "What's that supposed to—"
Before I could finish, he reached back with a quick flick of his hand and stuffed the apple into my mouth. It got stuck right between my teeth! I tried to protest, but I couldn't even get out a word!
"There!" Thoracks said. "That's better, ain't it?"
"*Mmmfffmnggghn!*"
"Thought so."
He began whistling happily.

The dusty trail spread out behind us. The cart bumped and jostled through the Dungeonworld night. Firebugs danced lazily in the sky above us.
    I sighed a lonesome prairie sigh.
    This was going to be a long ride...

THE END

Made in the USA
Las Vegas, NV
13 July 2022